STEP INTO READING®

STEP 2 READING WITH HELP

DC SUPER FRIENDS™

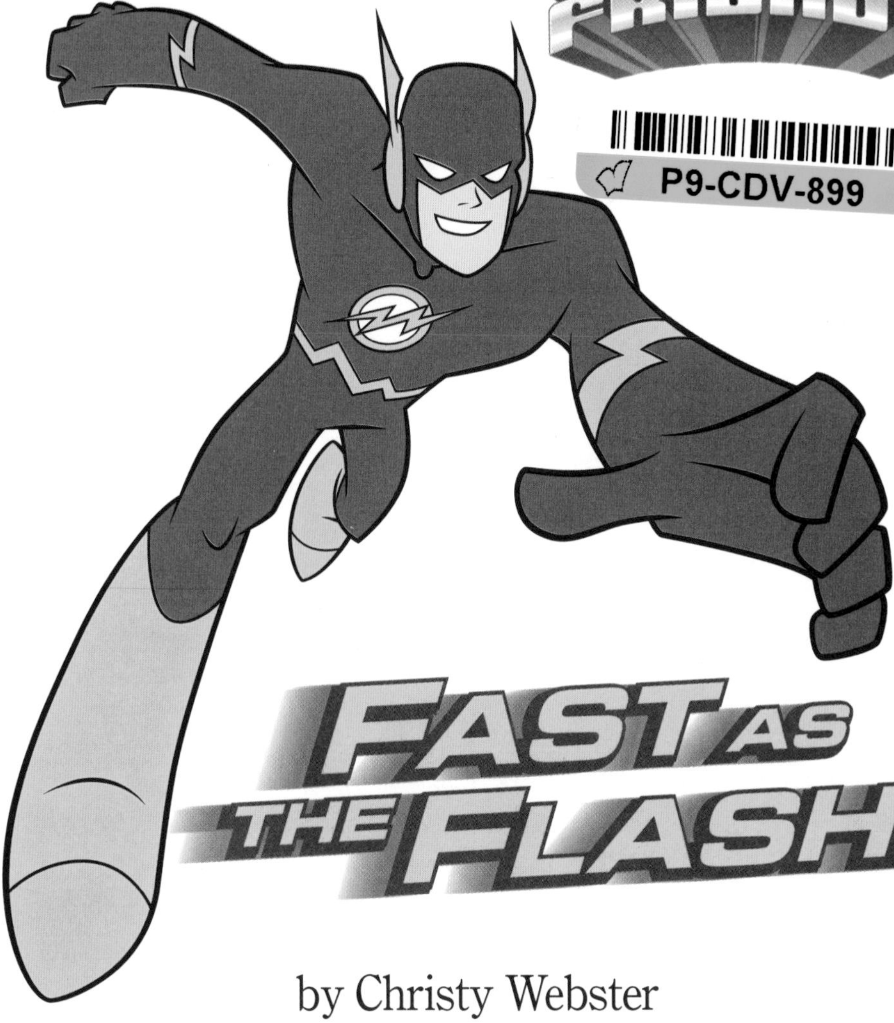

FAST AS THE FLASH!

by Christy Webster
illustrated by Erik Doescher

Random House New York

Meet The Flash.

He is a super hero.

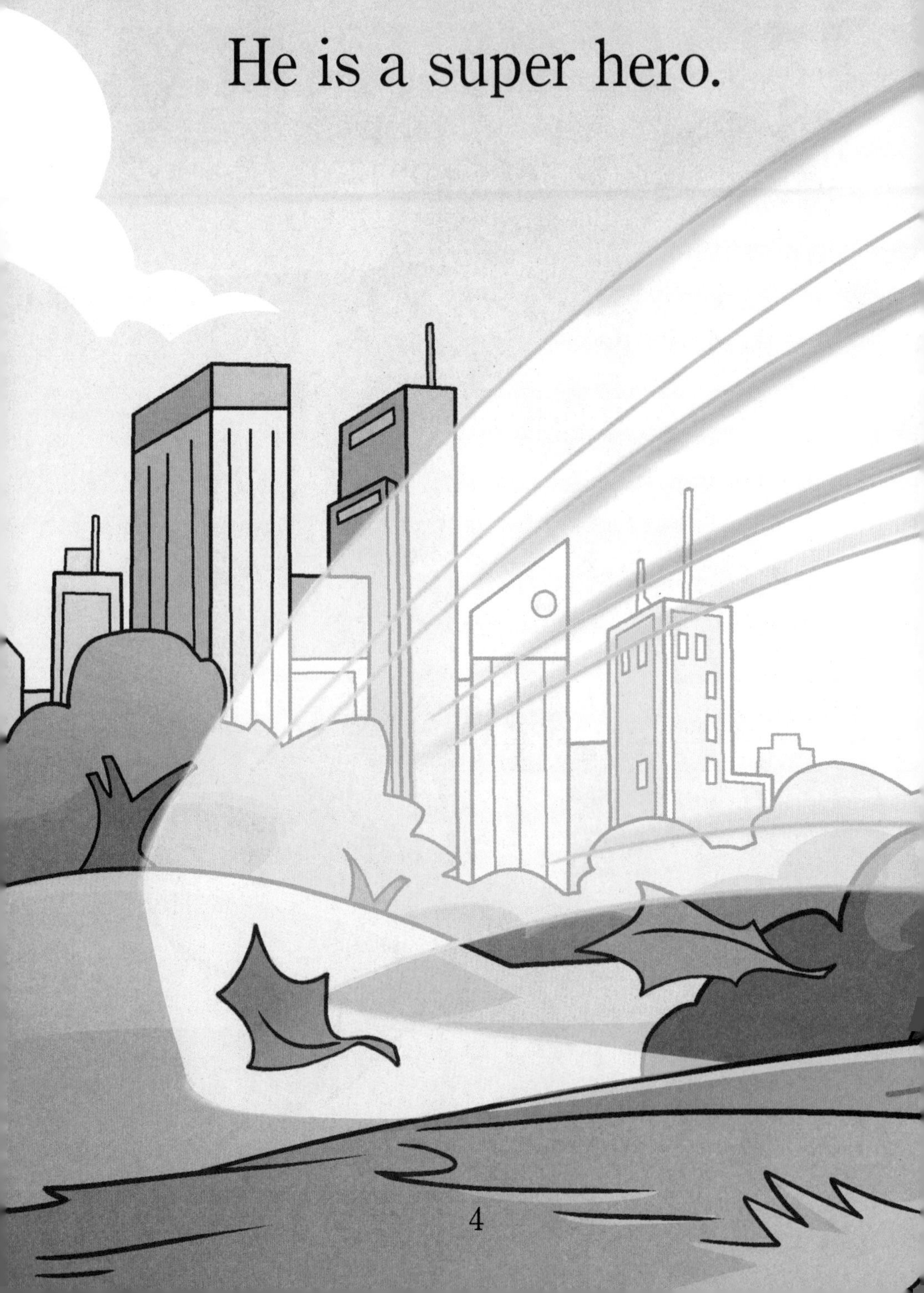

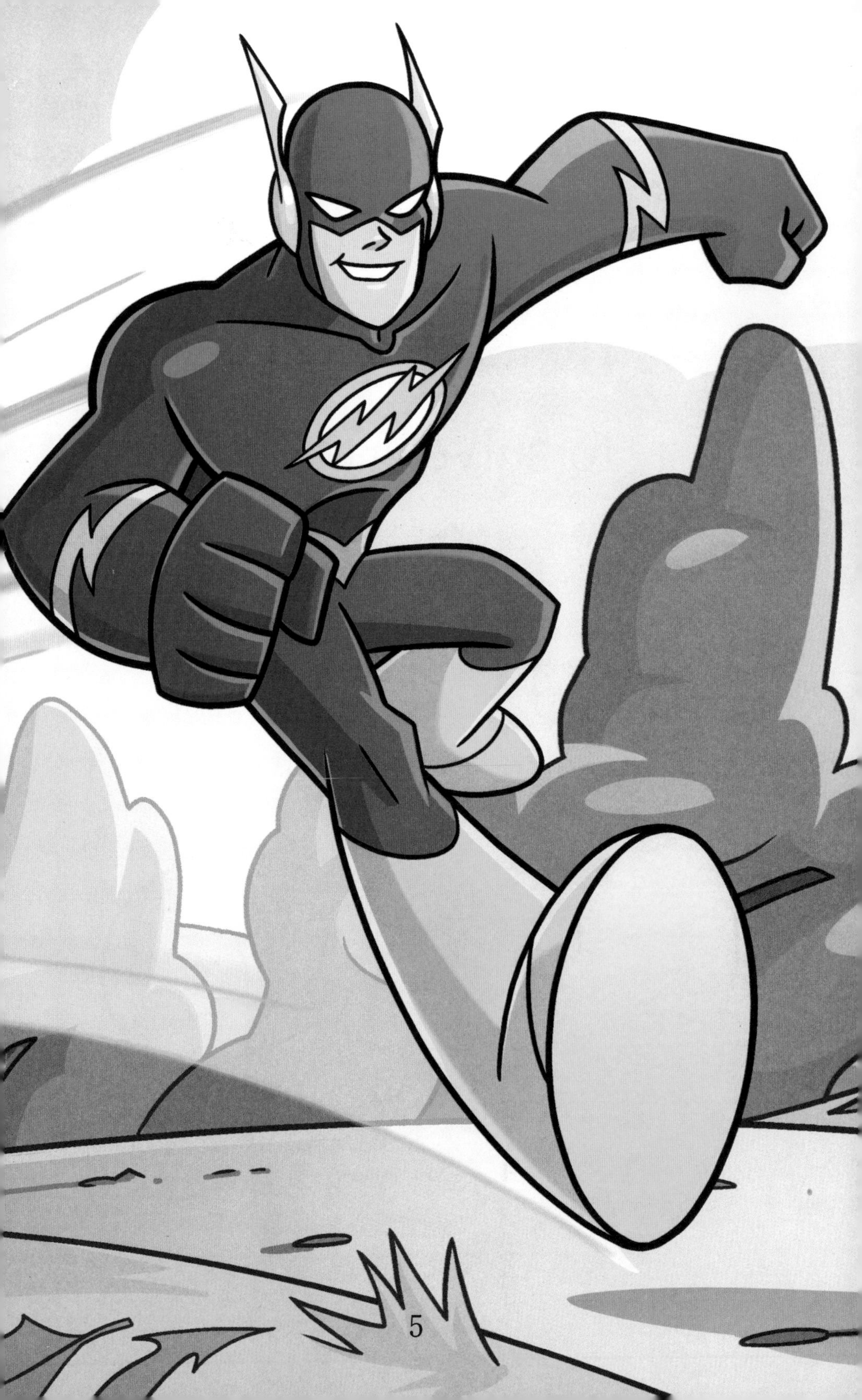

The Flash was
a policeman.
He used science
to solve crimes.

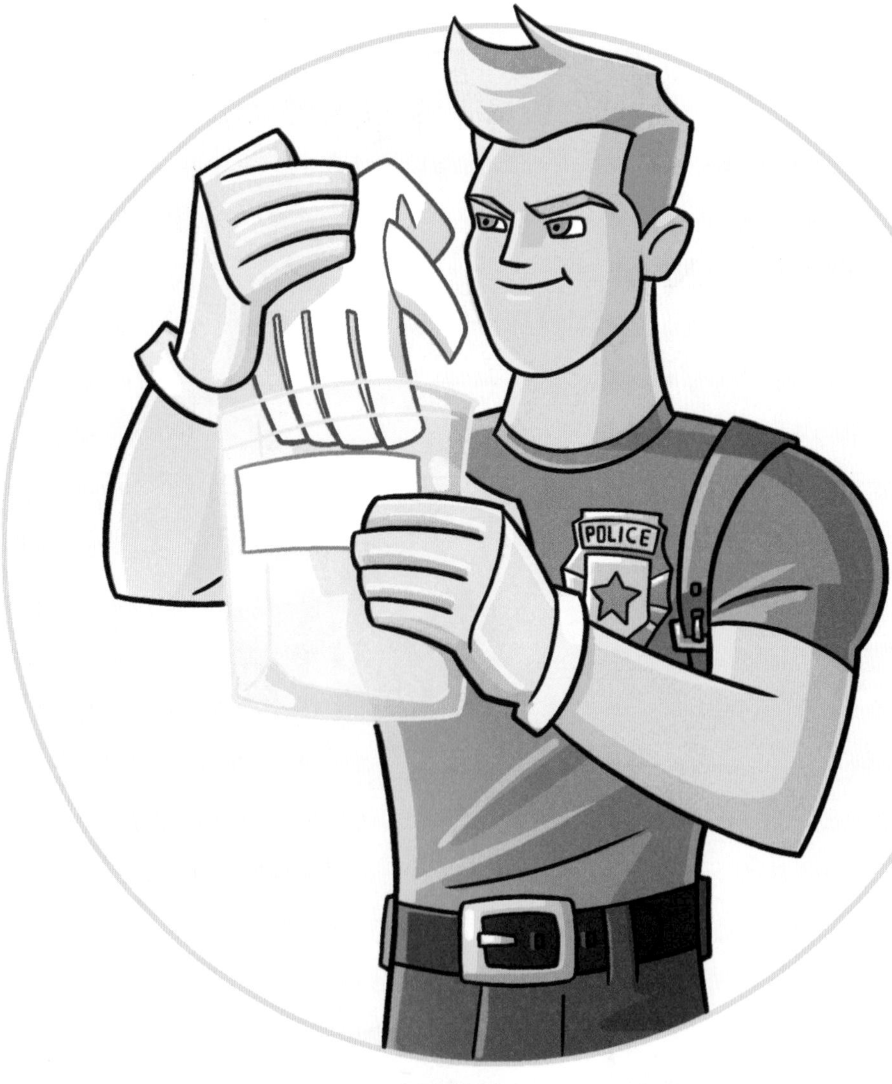
POLICE

A lightning bolt
hit his lab one day.
It smashed bottles.
Something spilled
on him.

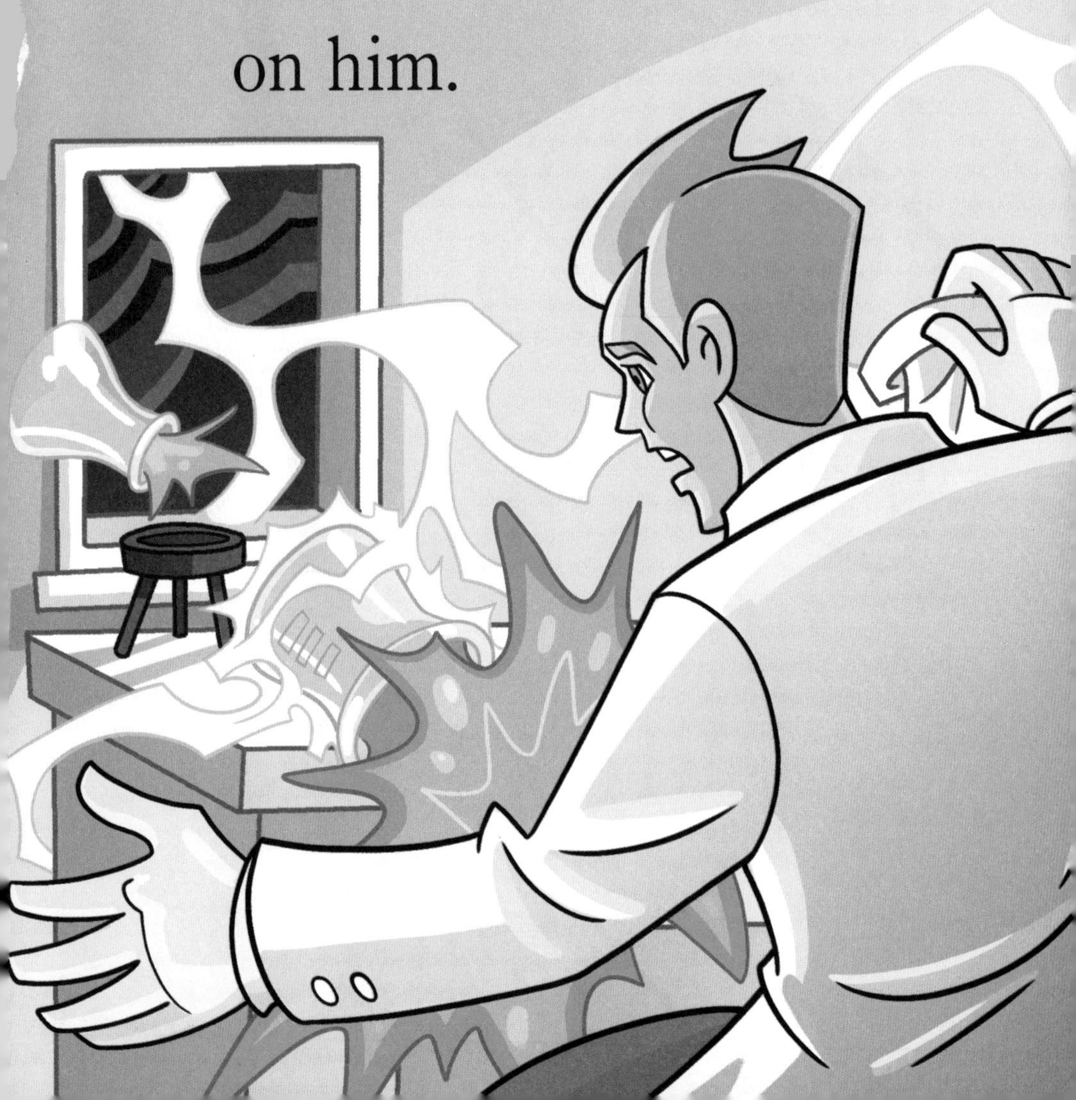

It made him
super-fast.

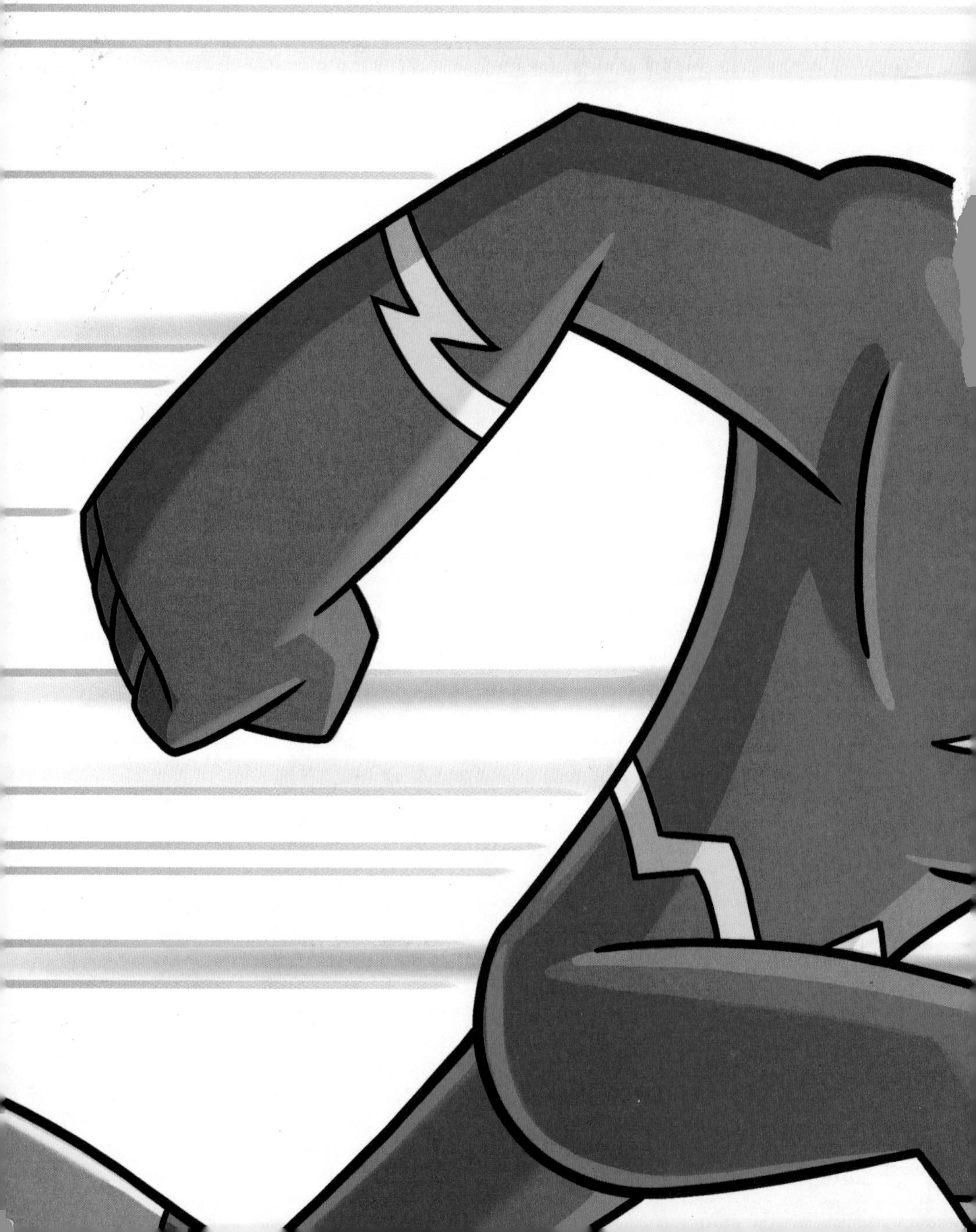

He became The Flash!

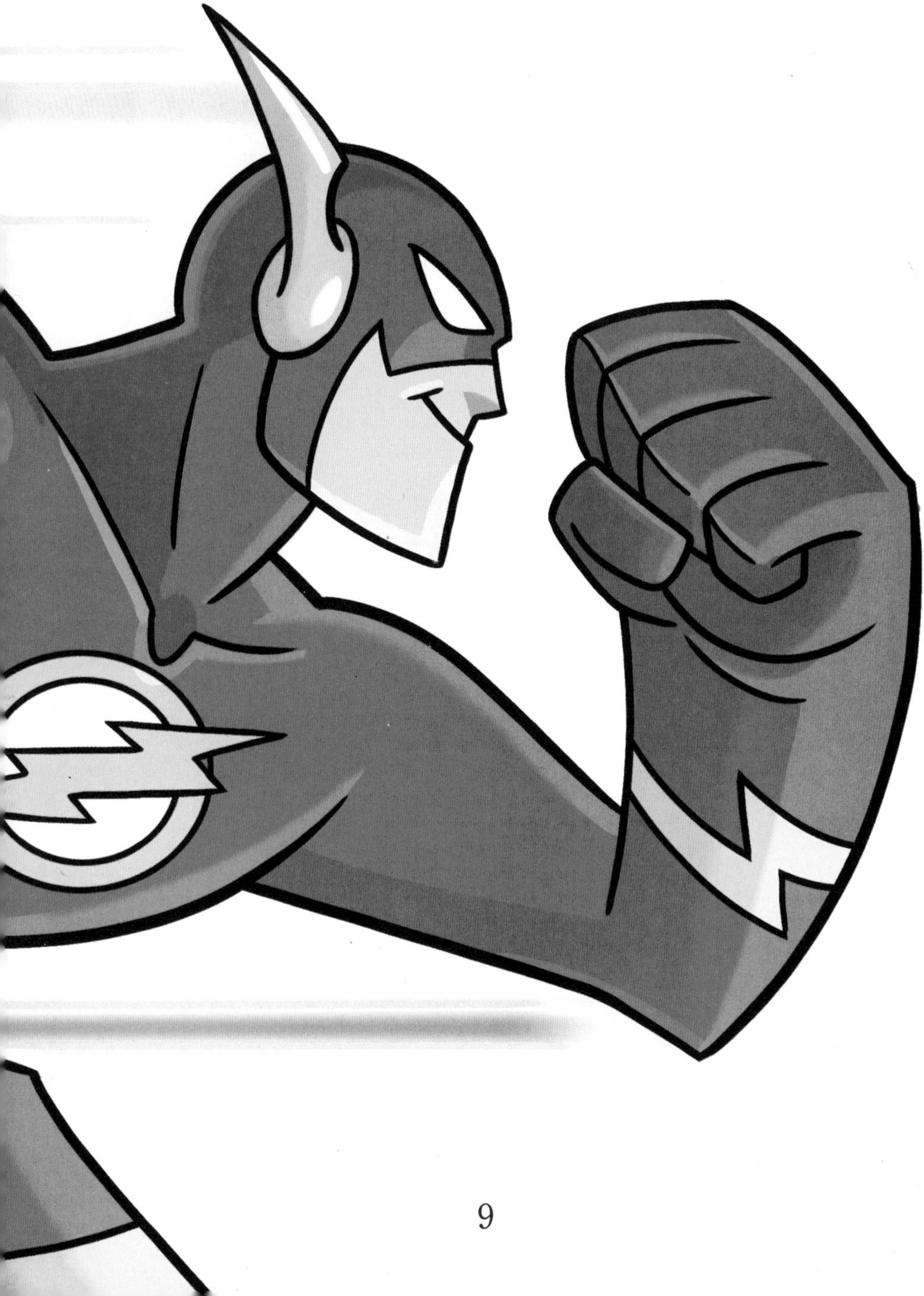

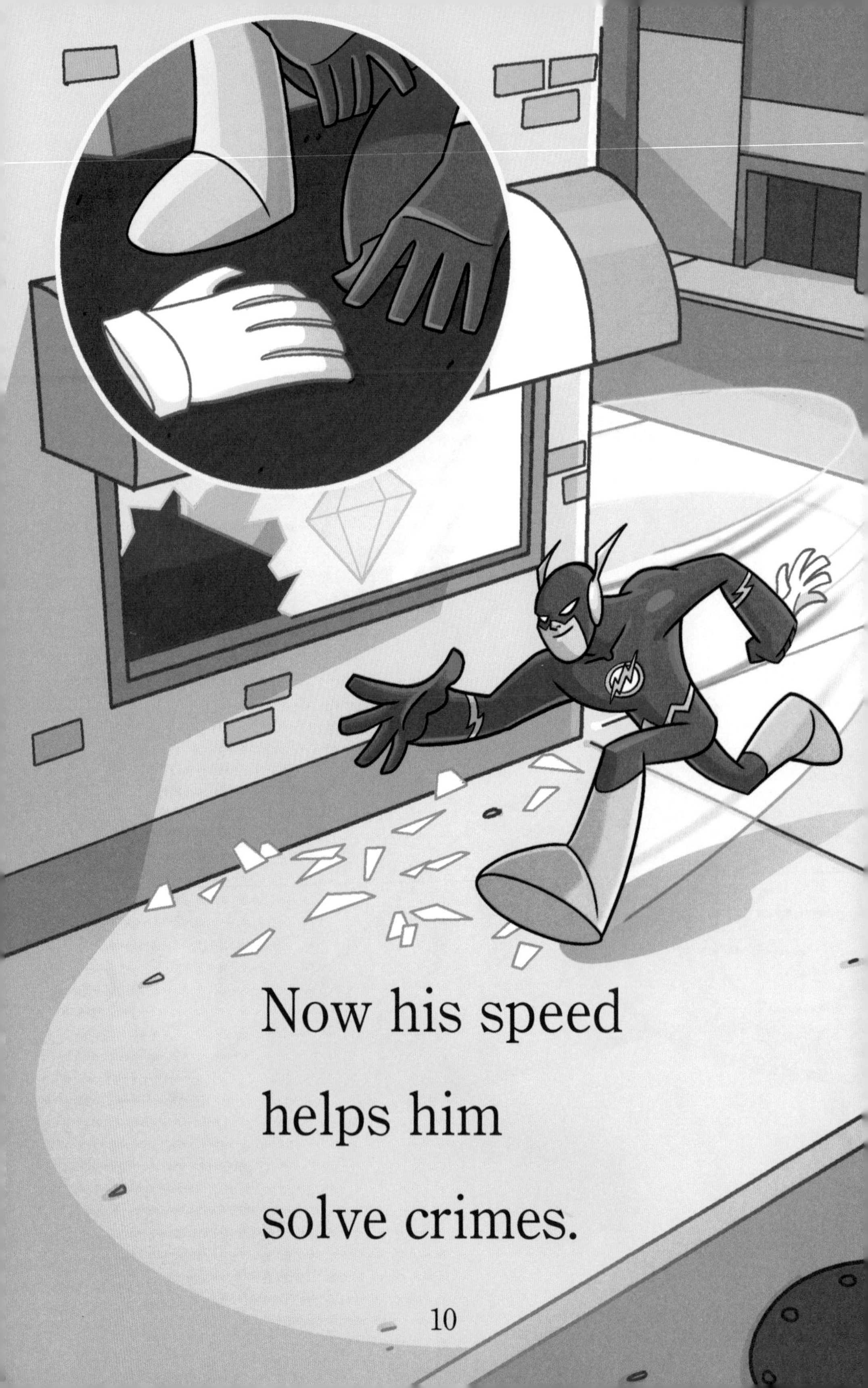

Now his speed
helps him
solve crimes.

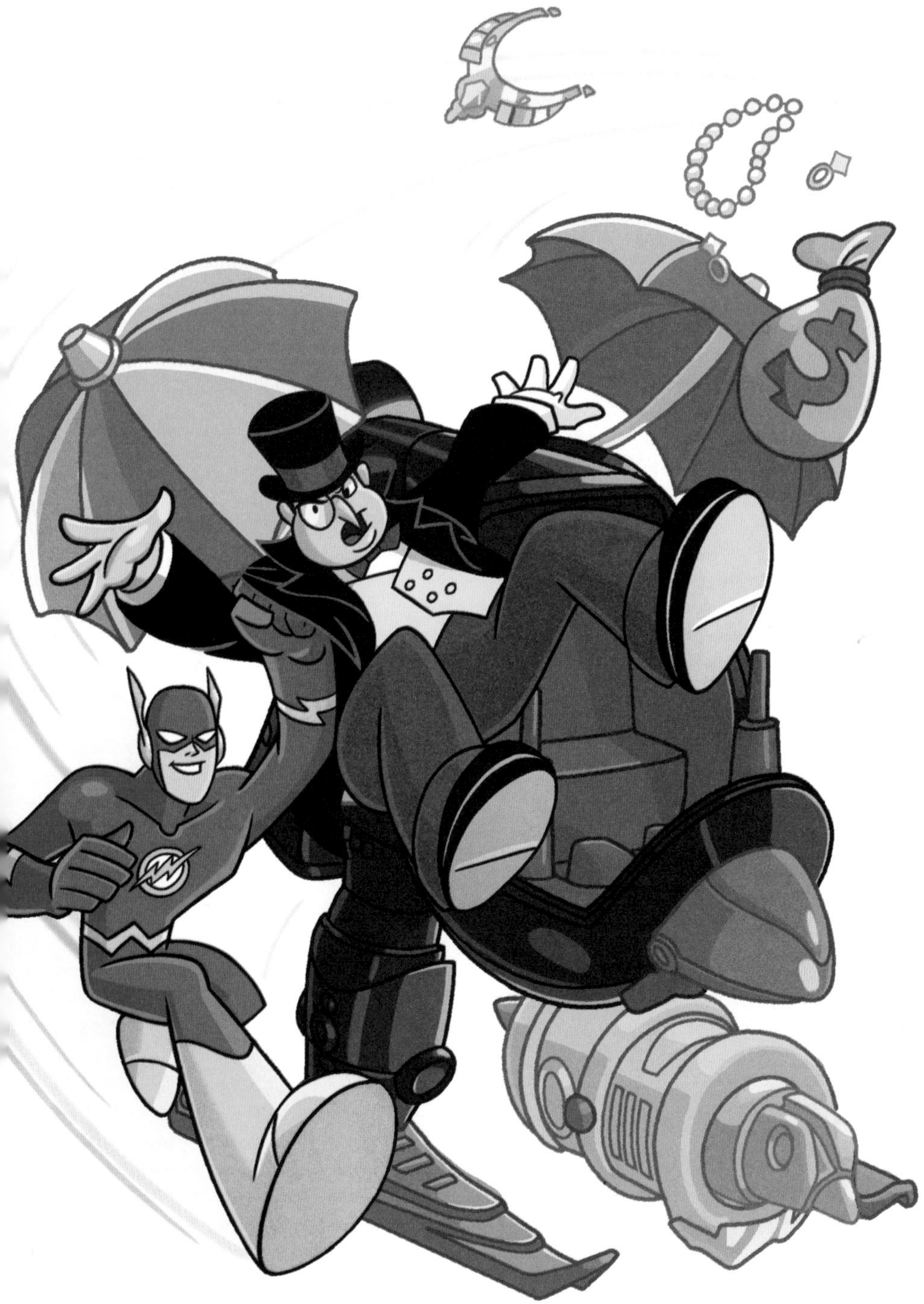

The Flash can run up buildings.

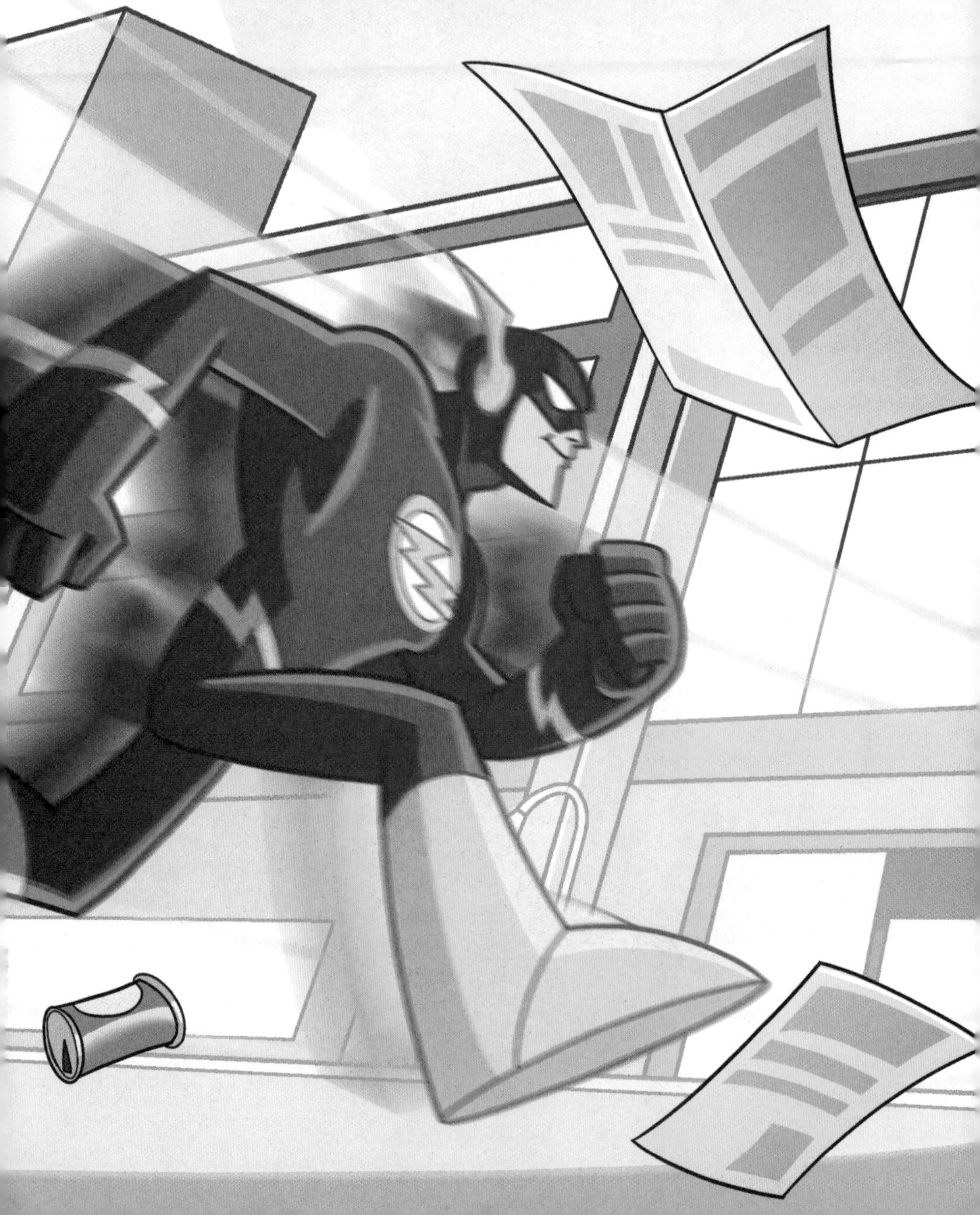

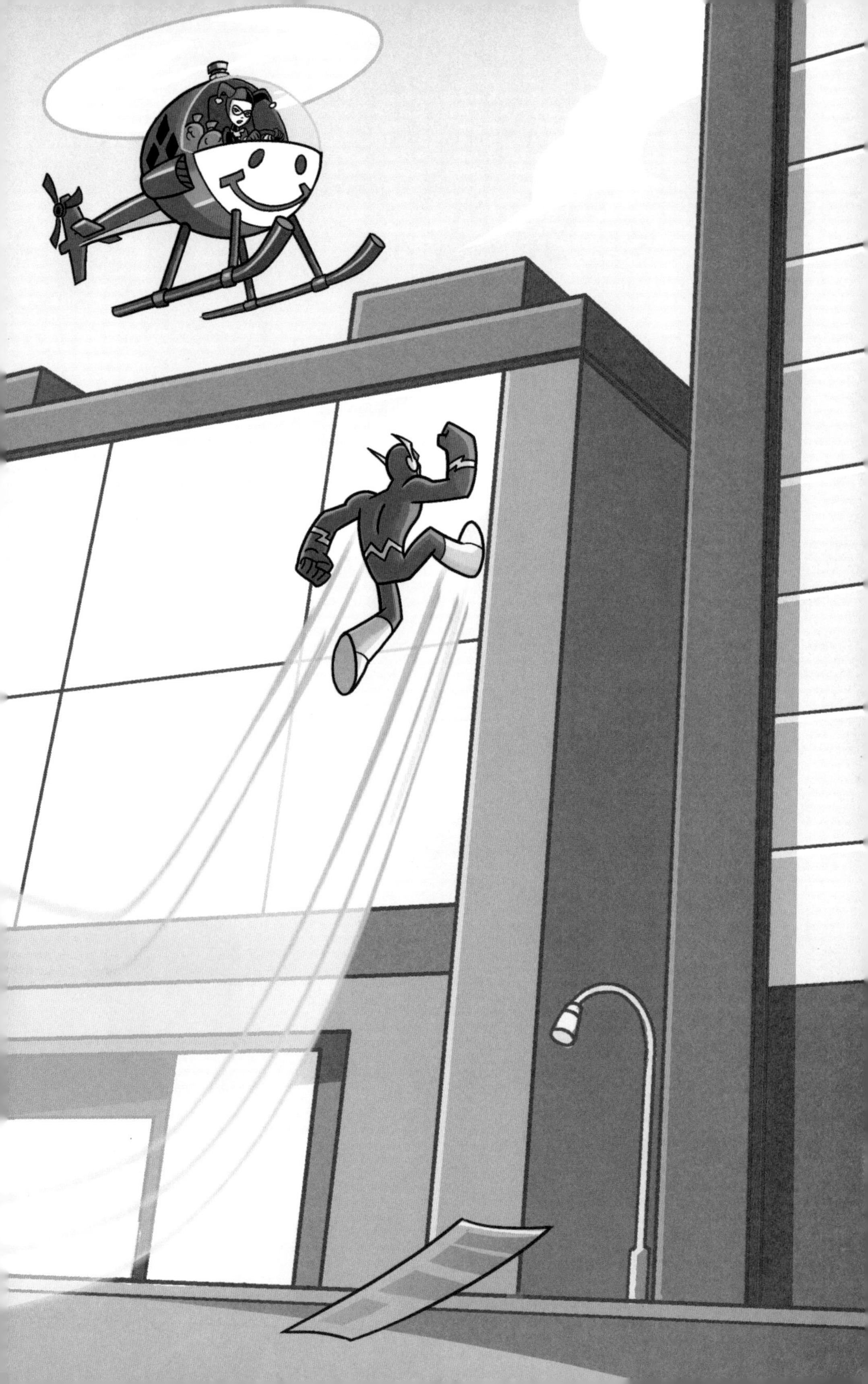

He can run
across the ocean
and create whirlpools.

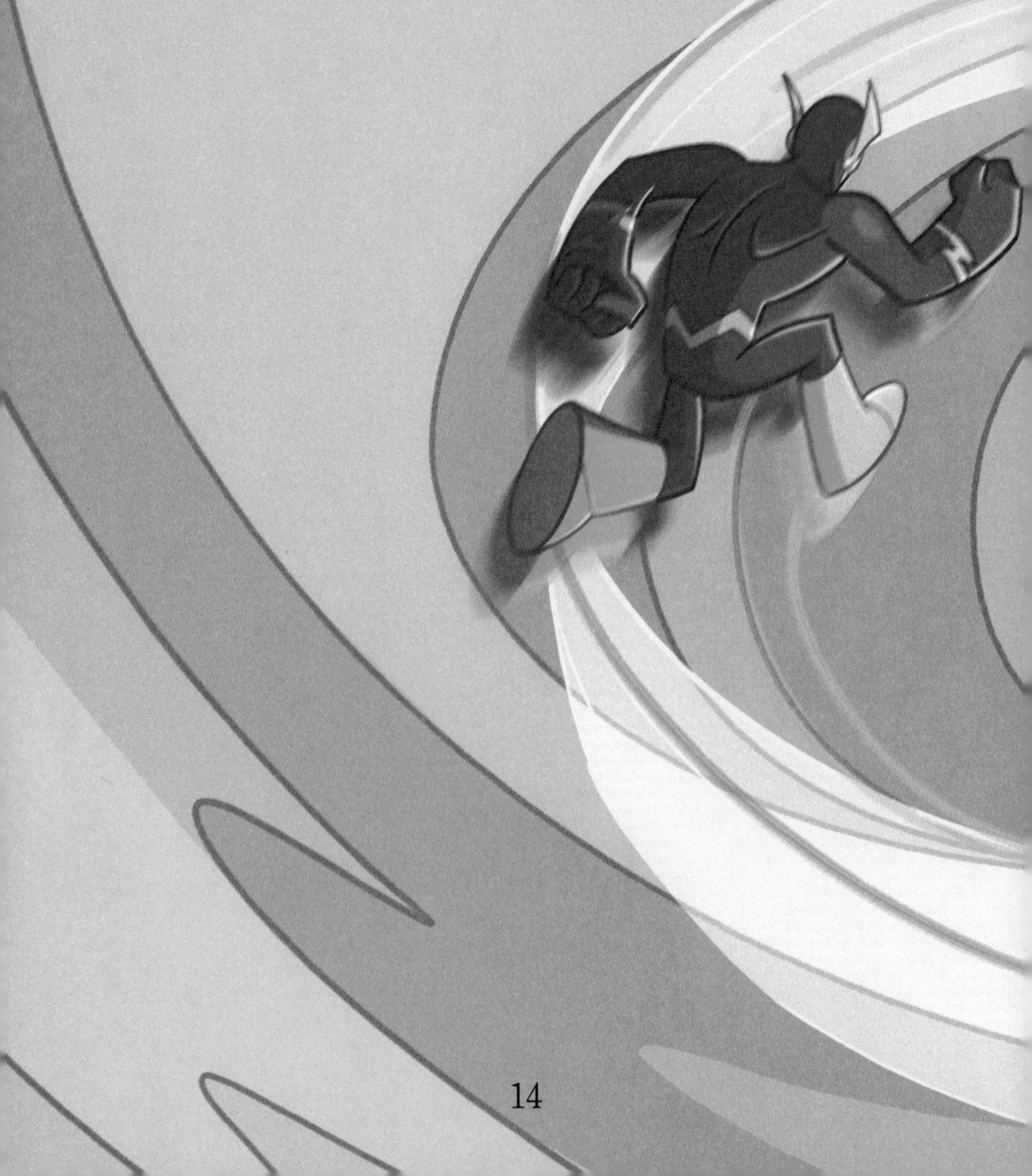

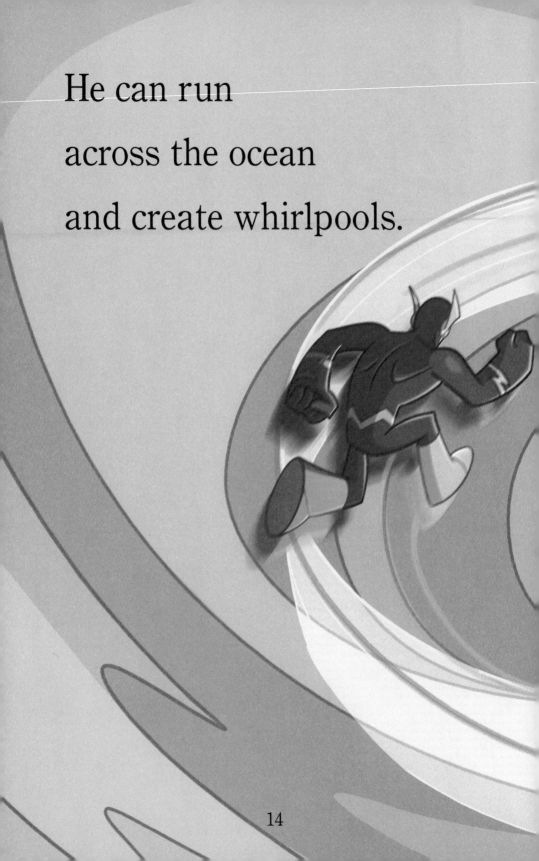

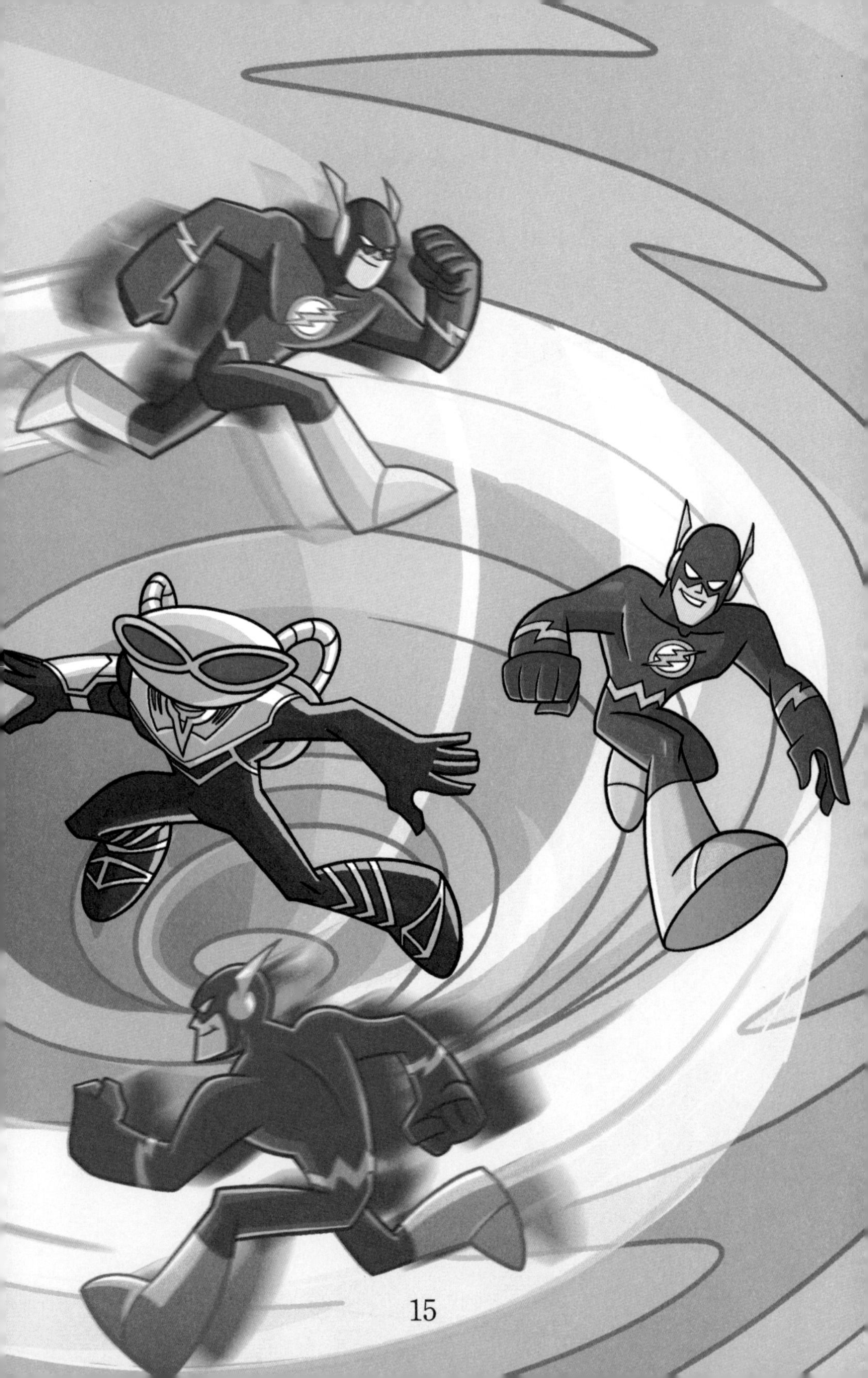

He can even run
around the world!

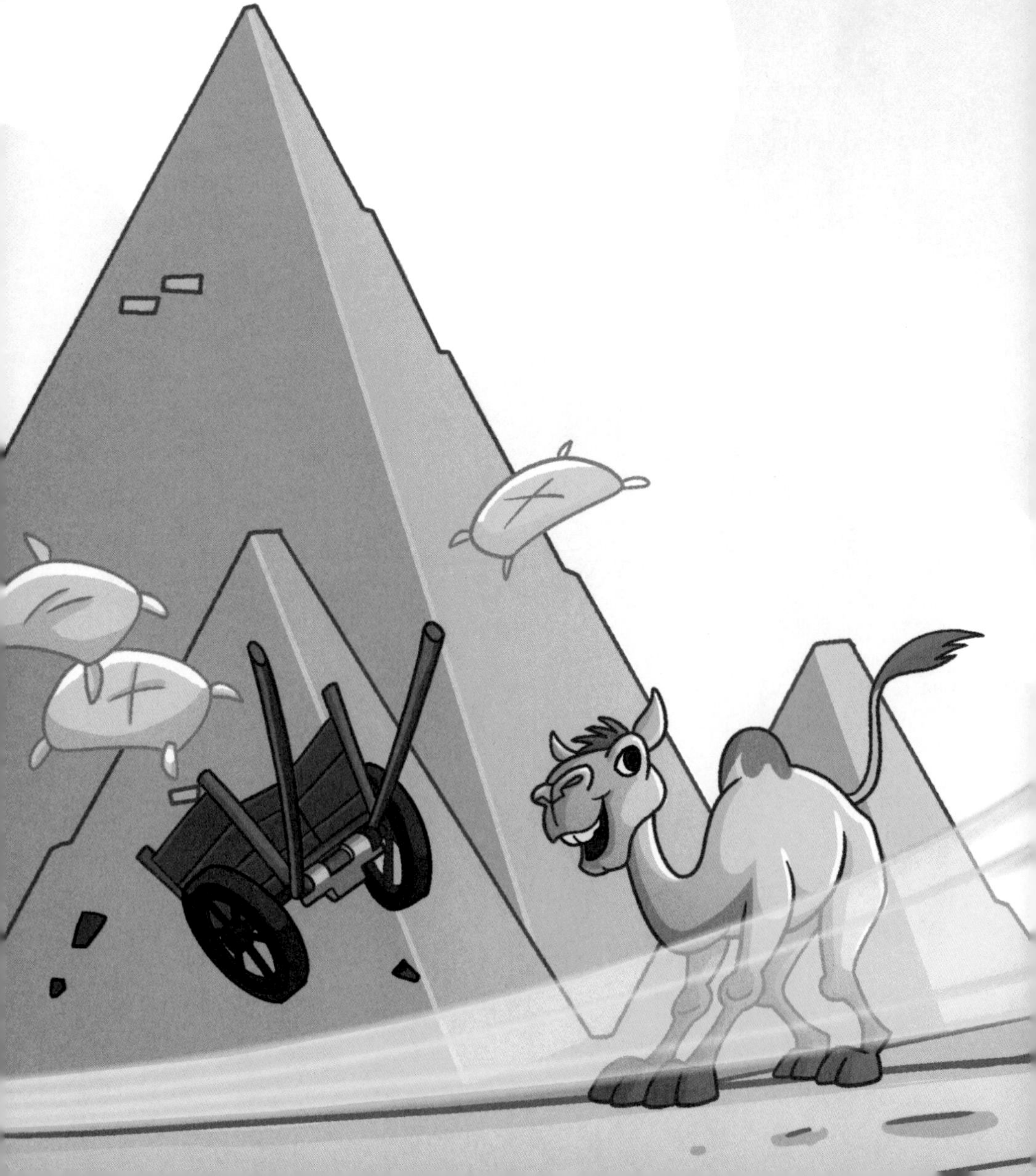

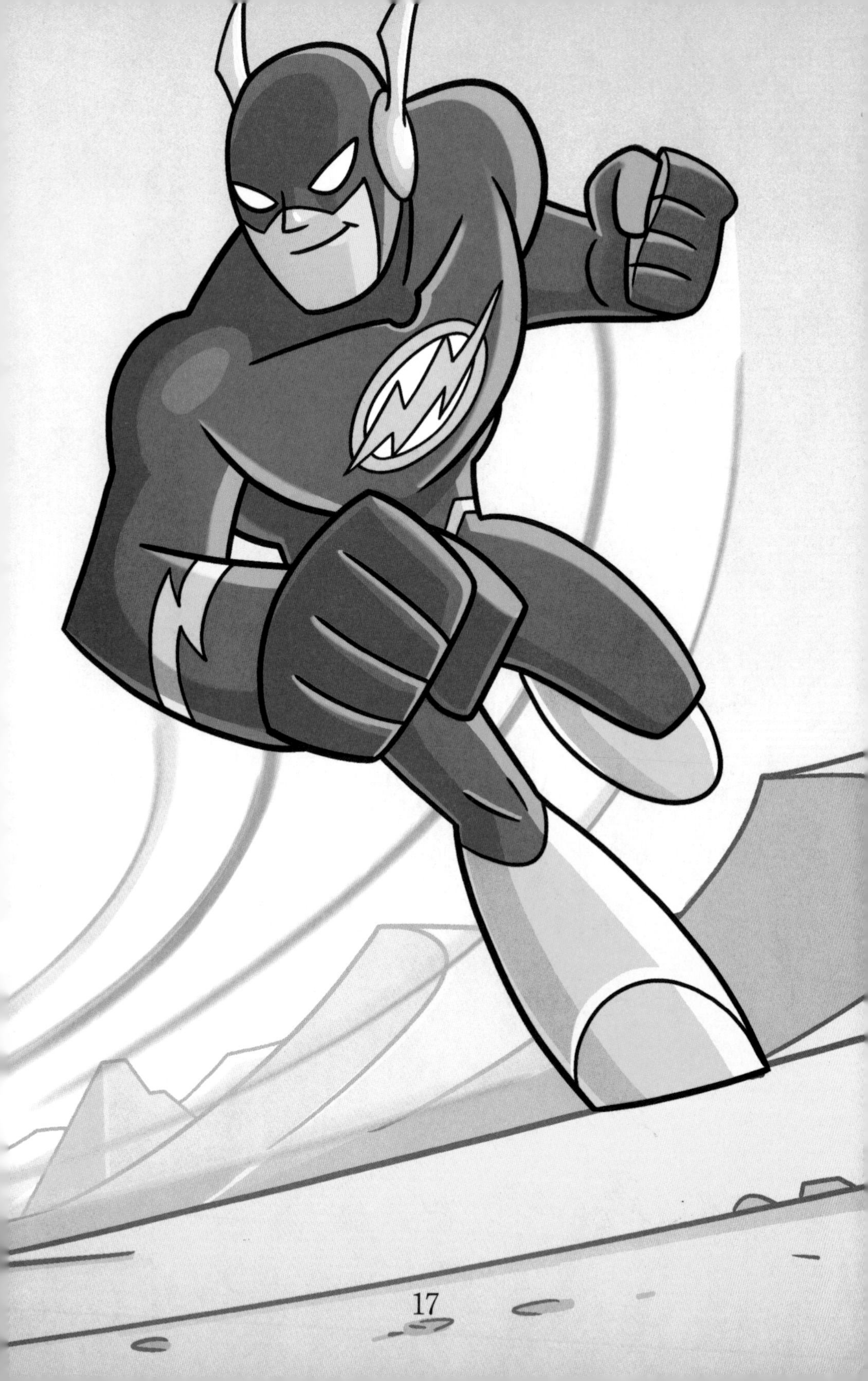

Cheetah is fast.

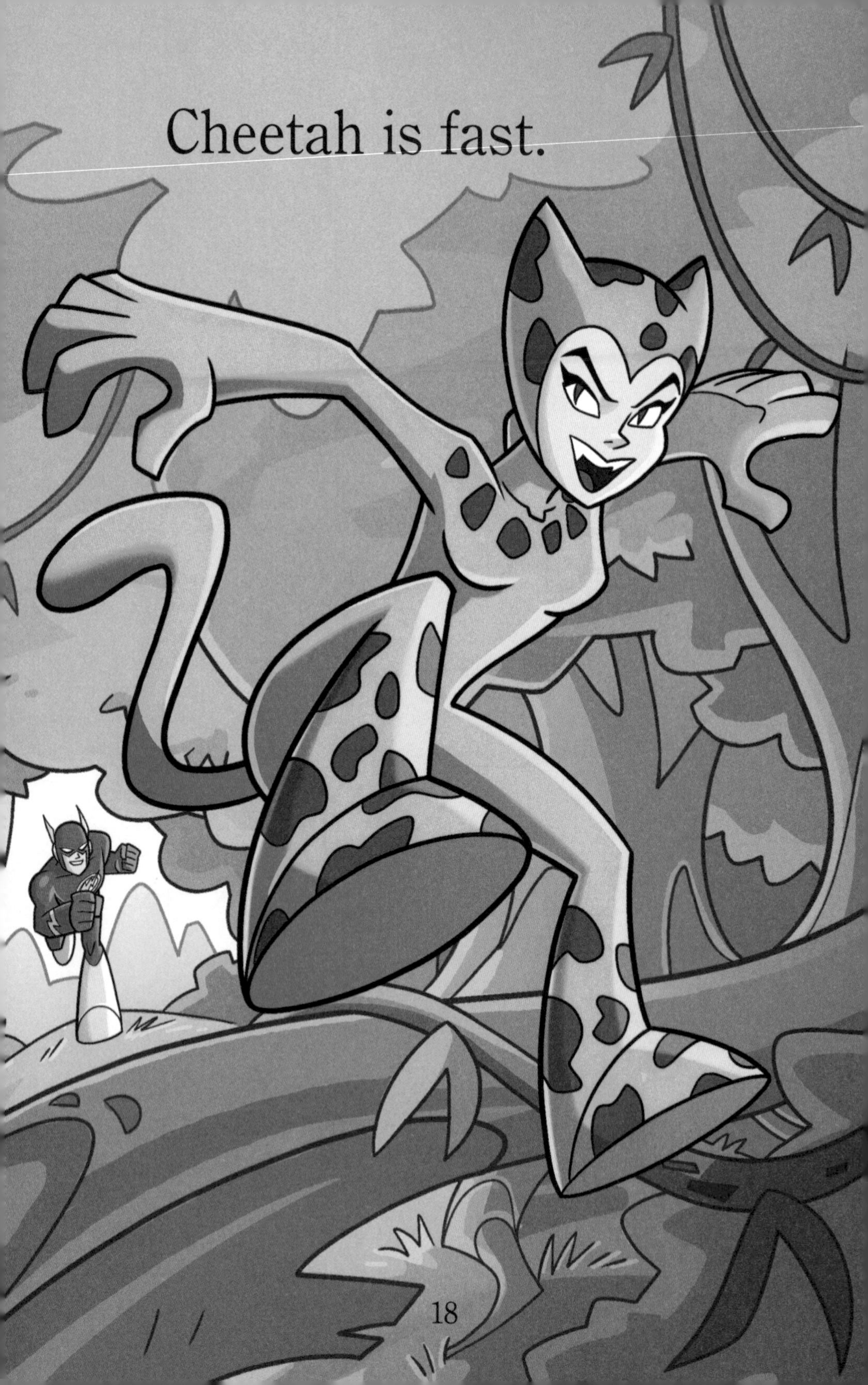

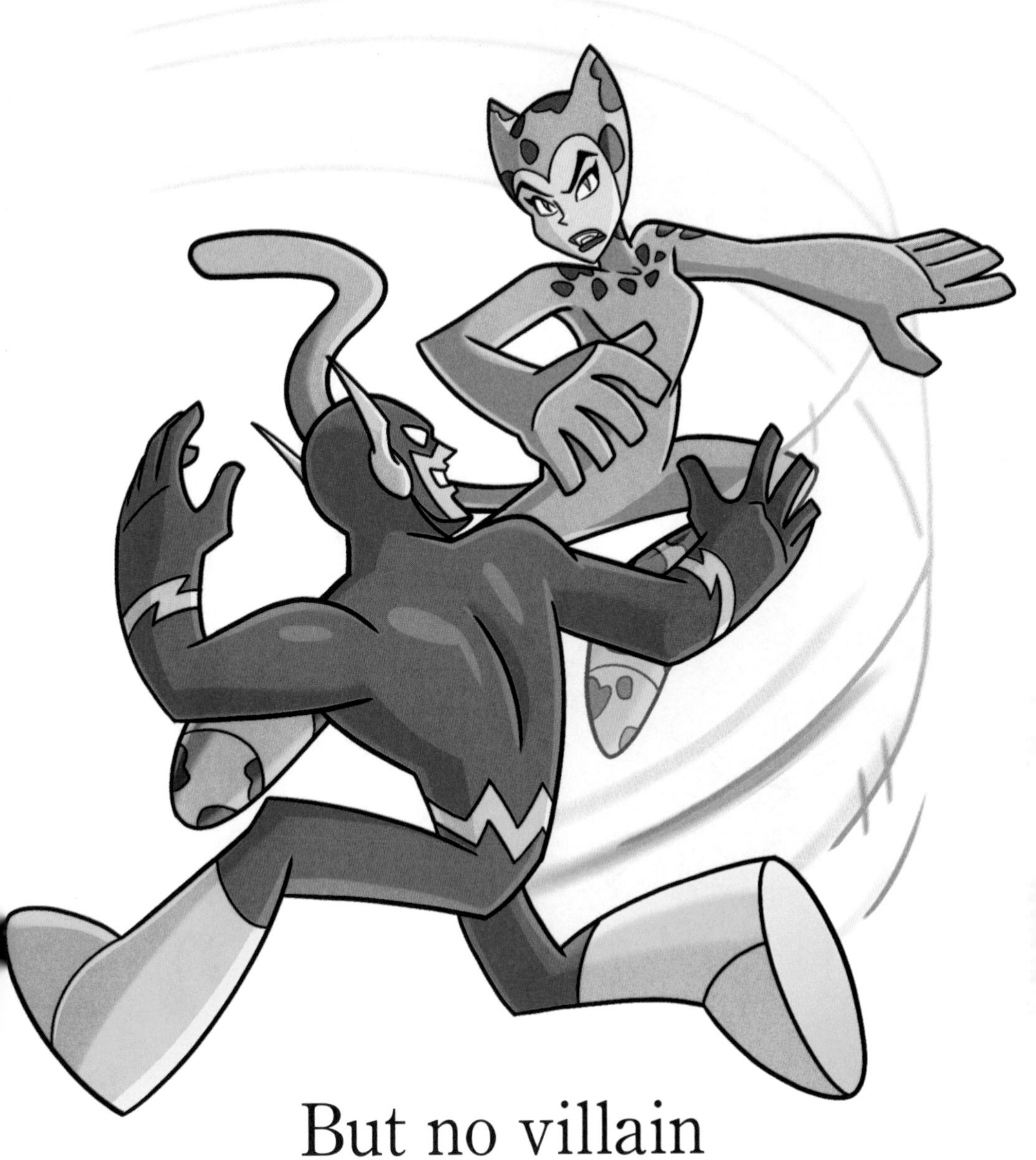

But no villain
can outrace
The Flash!

The Flash gets crooks to jail quickly.

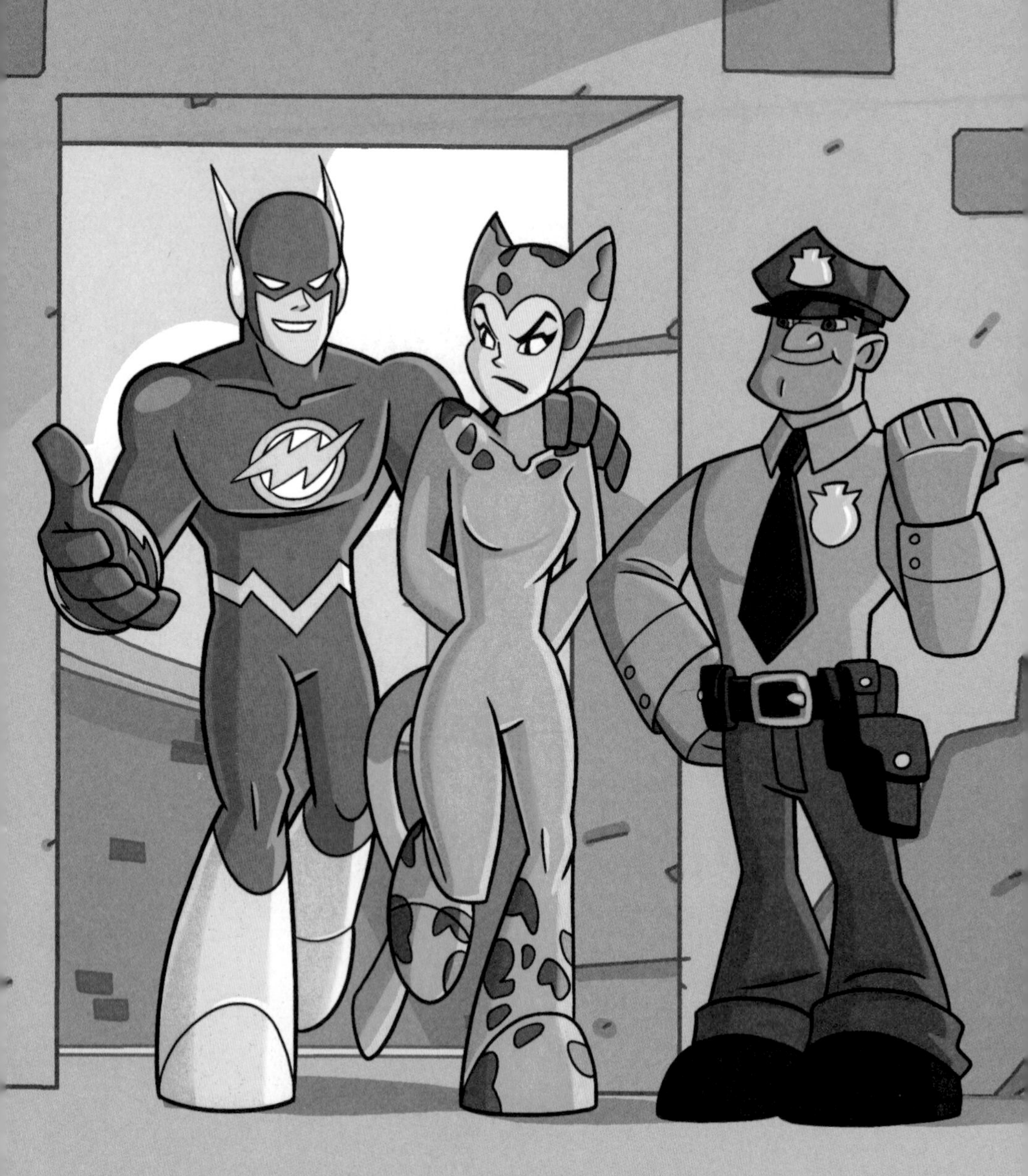

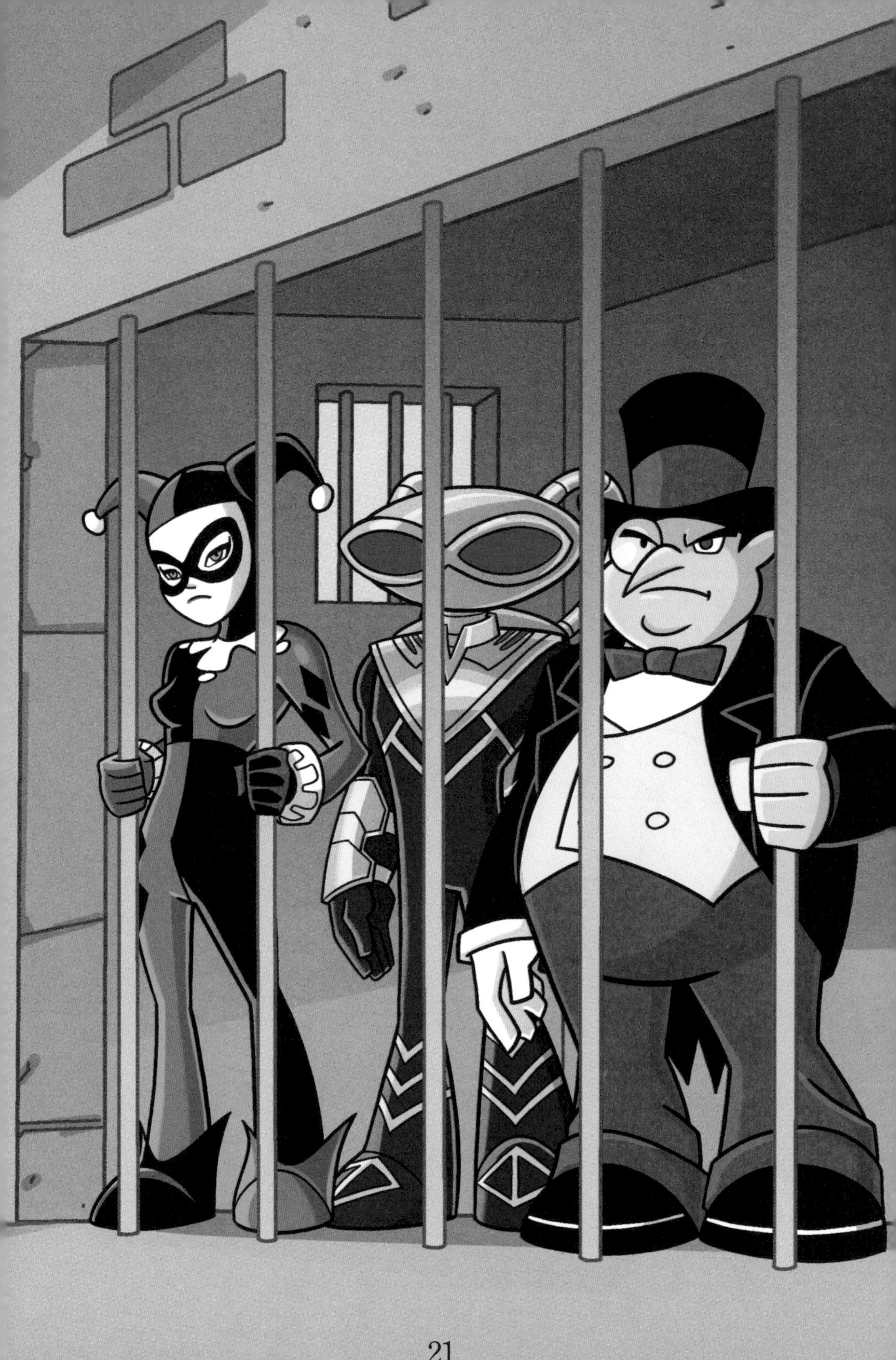

Who is as fast
as The Flash?

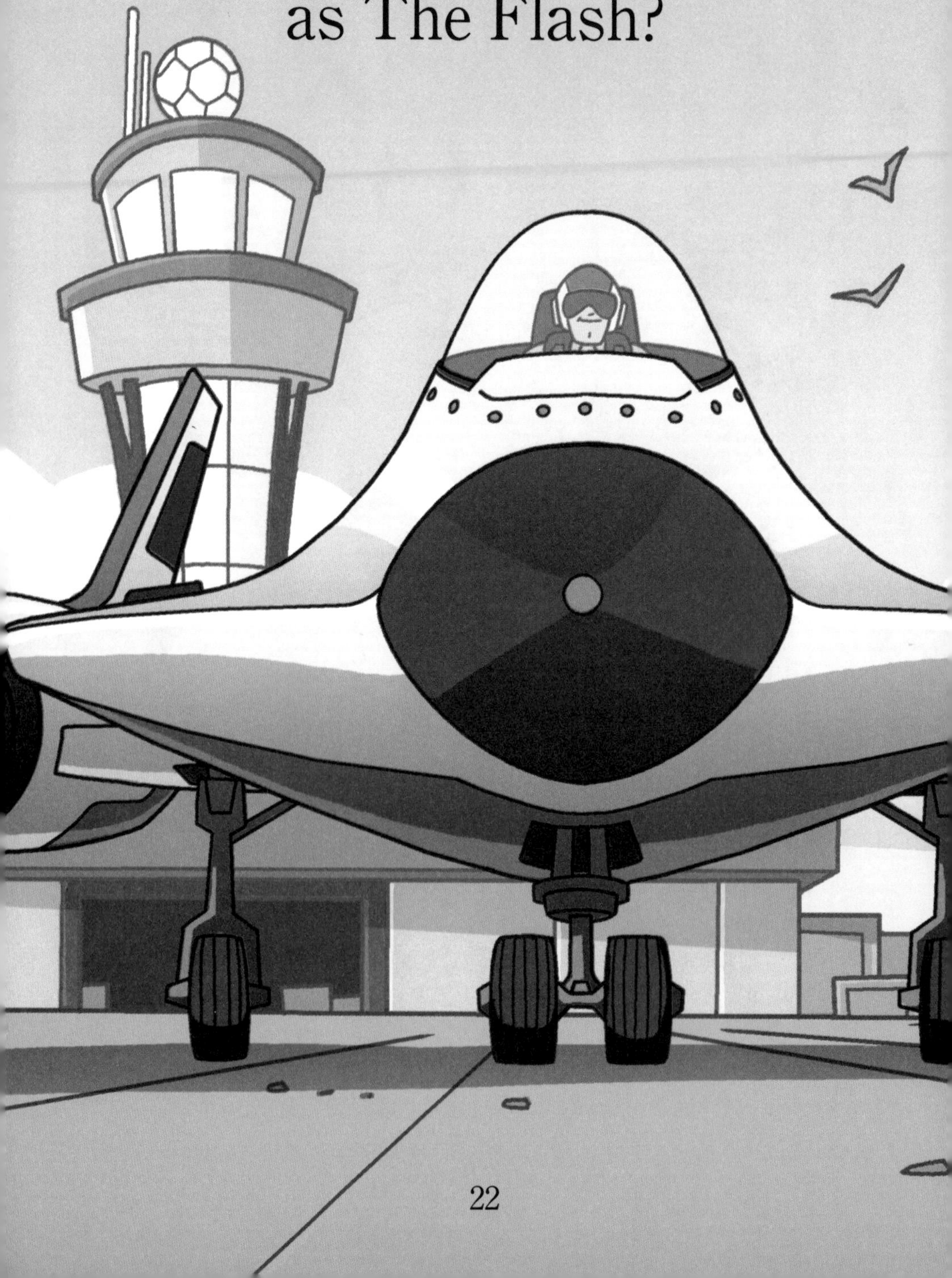

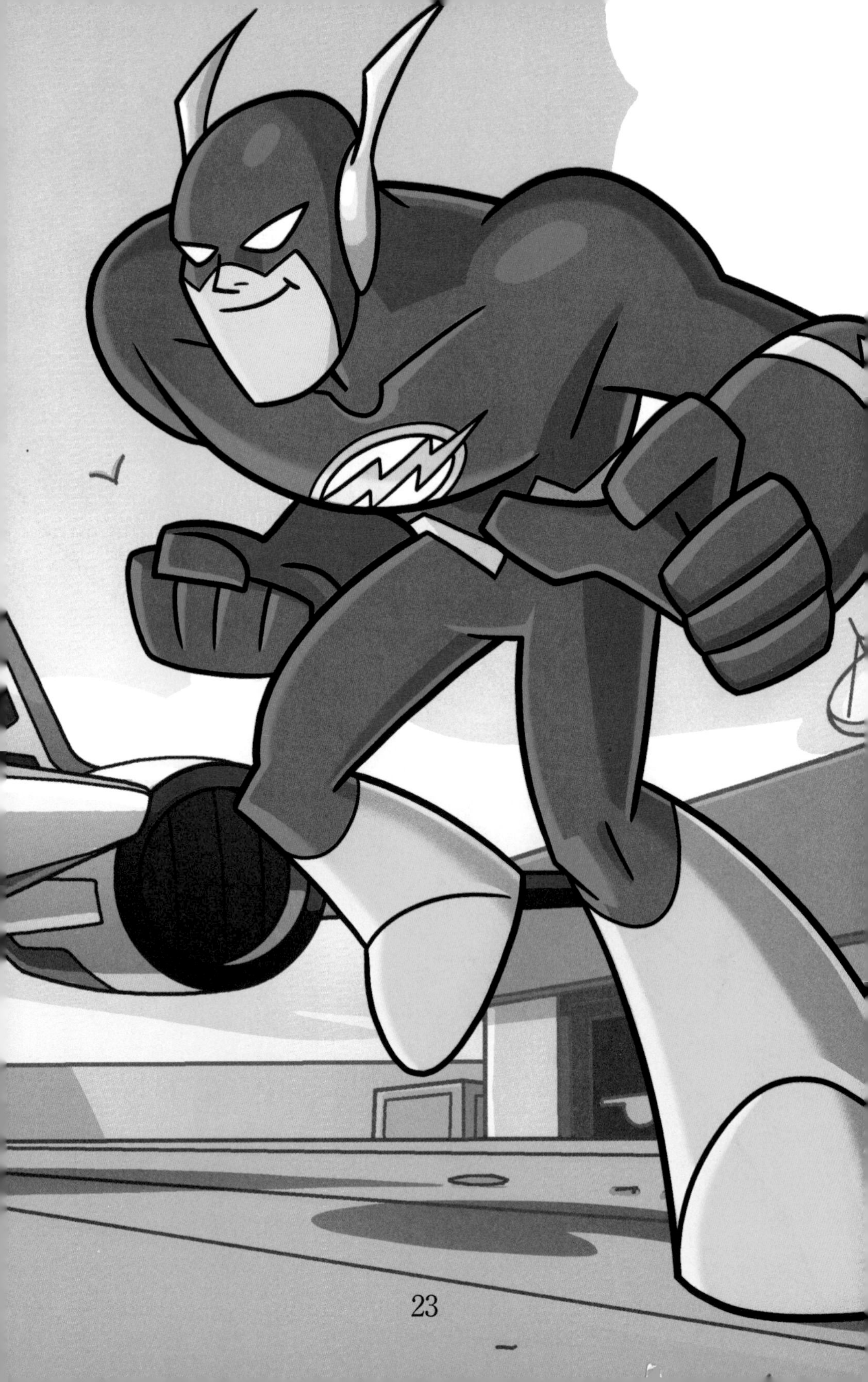

No one is as fast

as The Flash!

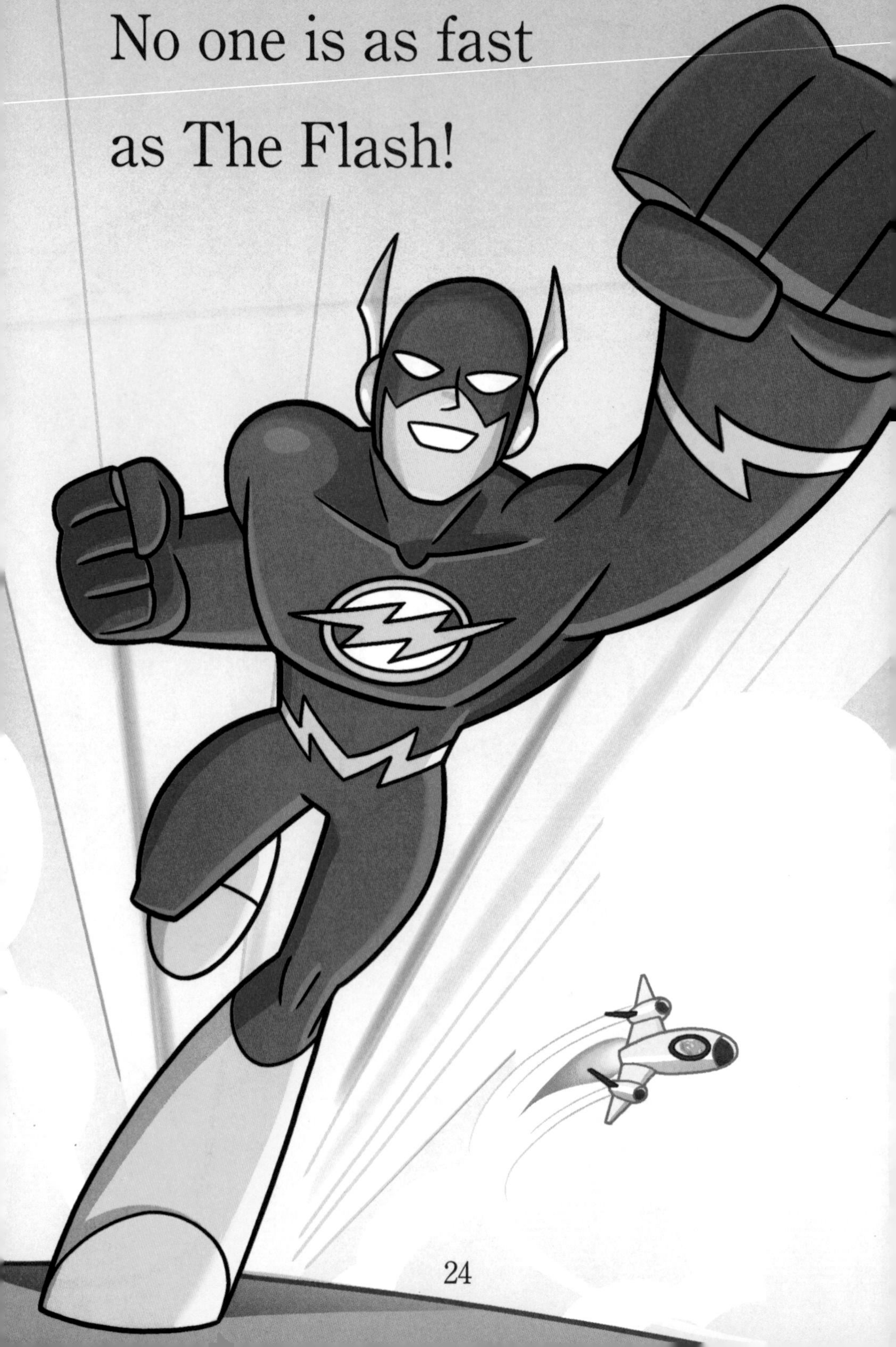